ONCE UPON A TRUFFLE

by Toby Talbot

illustrated by Michael Horen

Cowles Book Company, Inc.
New York

SBN 402-14004-4

Library of Congress Catalog Card Number 78-118914
Cowles Book Company, Inc.
A subsidiary of Cowles Communications, Inc.
Published simultaneously in Canada by
General Publishing Company, Ltd.
30 Lesmill Road, Don Mills, Toronto, Ontario

Printed in the United States of America

First Edition

Once Upon a Truffle

Author's note:

A truffle is a wrinkled fungus, usually black or brown, sometimes white, that grows underground and has a pungent aroma. It is a true French delicacy and prized by cooks and truffle lovers for preparing sauces, stuffings, and other pleasures of the table.

Pierre was a champion truffle-pig who lived in the town of Périgord in France.

Each November, and all through the winter, Pierre's master, Monsieur Daumont, tied a leash around him and off they went to the woods to hunt for delicious truffles. There, Pierre would nose around among the roots of oak trees until he caught a whiff of a truffle.

Then he would burrow away in
the ground until he uncovered
the little wrinkled plant.

At once Monsieur Daumont
would swoop down, seize the
truffle, and toss an ear of corn,
a potato, or a piece of cheese
to Pierre.

And always he said, "Good boy, Pierre."

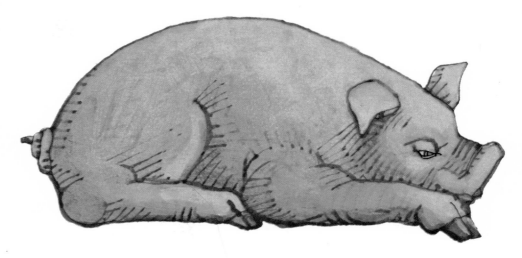

Now, Pierre, like many fat creatures, was
an easygoing, jolly sort, but all those years
of truffling without so much as a taste
finally began to get him down. He lost his
appetite and grew melancholy and listless.
Night after night he dreamed about sinking
his teeth into rich, black truffles. But when
he awoke from his dream he was always
chomping on an empty mouth. Forlorn
though he was, he tried to hide his
feelings.

"Maybe it will pass," he thought as he
poked around in the ground.

But some things don't pass. They just get worse. And by and by even Monsieur Daumont took heed.

"I wonder what's ailing Pierre," the farmer said to his wife one morning.

"He does seem pale, and he hardly smiles these days," Madame Daumont agreed.

Pierre listened miserably. How ashamed he was of his strange cravings. After all, he belonged to a noble line of truffle-pigs, with not a whiner in the lot.

"Somehow he's lost his lust for life," Monsieur Daumont went on.

"Maybe he needs vitamins," Madame Daumont suggested. "I read in a book on pig raising that in the United States they give even pigs vitamins."

"Bah!" scoffed Monsieur Daumont, who was an old-fashioned man.

The next day, after just picking away at his
breakfast, Pierre set out with Monsieur
Daumont for the truffle hunt as usual. The
air in the woods had a cold nip and the
acorns and dry autumn leaves crackled
and crunched underfoot. It was a lucky
day, and Monsieur Daumont's truffle
basket was soon full. As they were
heading home, Pierre sniffed out another
truffle.

After digging it up, he stood by patiently,
waiting for his master to take it.

"The basket can't hold any more,"
Monsieur Daumont said. "You eat it,
Pierre."

Pierre didn't have to be told twice. He snatched the dear morsel and gobbled it up. A wave of ecstasy rippled over him.

"Mmmm . . . that's just what the doctor ordered," he sighed blissfully.

It was like an injection of happiness. At once he perked up and his eyes glowed.

"Aha!" shouted Farmer Daumont.
"So that's your problem, Pierre.
You've dug for years
and never a nibble."

Pierre blinked and hung his head. His secret
was out. Truffles were indeed his weakness.

"Well, it's logical," Monsieur Daumont said.
"How long can one be so near and yet
so far?"

Farmer Daumont had a tendency to sprinkle
his conversation with proverbs the way
others sprinkle their food with salt. He went
on to add: "As they say, a bird in the hand
is worth two in the bush. Or, a truffle in the
mouth is worth two in the ground."

When they got home, Monsieur Daumont called a family conference with Madame Daumont.

"Wife," said he, "the time has come for us to repay Pierre for his long years of service."

"But he has everything a pig could want," Madame Daumont protested. "Three square meals a day, plenty of fresh air and exercise, and his work . . ."

"Don't argue," declared her husband. "I say, let him eat truffles!"

And with these words a new era began for Pierre: a life of truffle eating. All his food was garnished with them, his corn, his scraps, his milk.

His days were leisurely now—he never went out to hunt. But such a keen nose as his could not go to waste, so the Daumonts decided to make him their truffle taster. The moment Monsieur Daumont would come home from a truffling expedition, he'd tote the day's booty out to Pierre.

And Pierre with his trusty snout would sort out the most perfect, most pungent truffles for market and push aside the smaller ones. Those he ate. The scrawny ones were discarded.

"That's not fit for a pig," Monsieur Daumont would mutter.

The farmer then hurried off to market and bargained hard with merchants who came all the way from Paris to buy truffles. For there are truffles and then there are *truffles.* The most flavorful come from Périgord. When Monsieur Daumont came home, the money pouch tied around his belly would be so stuffed with bills that his shirt bulged. He soon became known as the most excellent truffle dealer in that region.

Madame Daumont, in her gratitude to Pierre, took to preparing special dishes for him. Truffle dishes.

"Pierre, *mon cher*," the good lady said one day at lunch, "I have a little treat for you." And she placed before him a dish of partridge cooked with truffles.

"Don't mind if I have a snack," thought Pierre as he smacked his lips and dug in.

"Formidable," said he to himself and polished it off to the last bone.

On other days, Madame Daumont made *pâtés de foie gras,* truffled sausages, and duck with truffles. Pierre, a true gourmet, devoured all the delicacies. He served as Madame Daumont's inspiration. Needless to say, he grew fatter and fatter and was melancholy no more.

Word spread among the Daumonts' neighbors about the goodies that streamed out of their kitchen. Before long, Madame Daumont, a shrewd and thrifty woman, decided to go into the restaurant business. Over their front door Monsieur Daumont hung a sign with a pig painted on it and the name *Chez Pierre.* The townspeople flocked to the new restaurant to taste the truffle masterpieces.

One fine day, a somber-looking gentleman appeared at their door. When he saw Pierre sunning himself beneath the sign he said:

"This must be the place."

Pierre opened one eye and studied the stranger. By his elegant clothes

Pierre guessed that he was from the city.

The man entered and Monsieur Daumont took his order for a truffle meal. The customer started with *pâté,* went on to goose stuffed with truffles, and wound up with truffles and ice cream. When he was through he burped with satisfaction, lit a cigar, and ordered a brandy. As he left, he handed Monsieur Daumont a calling card. It read: ''You have just served a meal to a Michelin representative.''

Now, as every Frenchman knows, Michelin representatives are men who tour all over France, eating meals in big restaurants, roadside inns, and little out-of-the-way taverns. The purpose of all this is to judge the quality of the restaurants and to give them ratings in the famous Michelin guidebook to all the hotels and restaurants in France. A place listed without stars is satisfactory. One star means that it's good, two stars that it's excellent, and three stars that it's supreme. Only a handful of restaurants gain the three-star distinction. But that year, when the new guidebook appeared, *Chez Pierre* had earned three stars!

Well, you can't imagine what that
did for the reputation of the Daumonts'
little restaurant. Serious eaters from all over
France began pouring in to savor the specialties of the
house. And, oh, how that house smelled! The fragrance
of sweet country butter, wine, garlic, and truffles could have
awakened hunger in a stone. And when the diners left, patting their
bellies contentedly, they'd nudge each other, point to the stout pig who
lazed around the kitchen garden, and whisper, "There he is, that's Pierre."

Business was so good that Monsieur Daumont decided to buy a wife for Pierre. She was a lovely creature. Her name was Henriette. Pierre fell in love with her as soon as he laid eyes on her.

"How gracefully she cocks her ears," he boasted to his friends, "and how she waddles when she walks!"

Henriette was a perfect wife. She didn't talk too much, and she loved her mate dearly, every inch of him. The marriage was soon blessed with a brood of beautiful piglets.

Pierre was now living in a pig's paradise. He gorged himself on truffles, soaked himself in hot and cold mud baths, had a doting wife to scratch his back and babies to carry on the noble family name. The only thing to mar his happiness was a little liver trouble from all that rich food.

But since neither men nor pigs are content with their lot for very long, Pierre one day found himself again falling into a black mood. Suddenly life had no meaning for him. He had so much time on his hands, and no desire for anything. Not even for truffles, or playing with his squeezable piglets. His hide grew dull, his expression cowlike, and he moped around a lot.

"Oh, woe," he brooded as he fanned a horsefly off his rump. "Why was I born? I'm just a flabby good-for-nothing."

Not even Henriette could cheer him up.

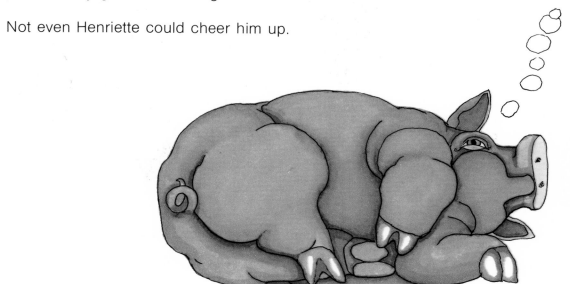

"What's bothering Pierre?"
Monsieur Daumont asked
Madame Daumont over
breakfast, pulling on his
moustache, as he always did
when puzzled.

"I can't imagine," she
answered, dipping her bun
into her coffee. "I hope he
hasn't caught a chill."

"Well, don't worry, dear," Monsieur Daumont said as he put on his beret
and kissed his wife. "We all have our ups and downs. But life must go on.
And now, I'm off to the truffle hunt. As they say, the early bird catches
the worm."

Upon reaching the door he noticed a wistful expression on Pierre's face. And the pig began sniffing around and moving his head from left to right.

"*Zut!* I've got it," cried Monsieur Daumont. "Pierre misses the hunt! He longs for the thrill of tracking down his own truffles, the crisp air, the mighty oaks, burrowing in the earth. Once a truffle hunter, always a truffle hunter."

Pierre's ears perked up, his heart beat fast, and he quivered from hide to hoof.

"By my snout," he thought, "you can say that again."

"Let's go, Pierre!" Monsieur Daumont called out. And away they tramped into the woods.

Well, from that day on Pierre never missed a day of truffle hunting, and more

often than not he'd bring home a choice truffle for his beloved Henriette.

The days turned to weeks and the weeks to months, and one fine day the postman delivered a letter from the Exclusive Circle of French Chefs.

Exclusive Circle of French Chefs
17 rue Divine, Paris 1ème

Monsieur Daumont and party are invited to the Annual Tasting and dinner to be held at 17 rue Divine on 3 April at 8 o'clock
R.S.V.P.

Since it was the end of March and the truffle-hunting season would not begin until next November, the Daumonts decided to accept the invitation.

On the morning of April 3, they packed a hamper full of food,
for no prudent French family travels without provisions.
Of course, Henriette and the piglets came along,
since Pierre couldn't bear to be parted from them.
By nightfall their train was in Paris.

A limousine was waiting at the railroad station to drive

the Daumonts and Pierre to the Exclusive Circle of French Chefs.

EXCLUSIVE CIRCLE OF FRENCH CHEFS

The members were seated around the table when the Daumonts arrived. They were wearing tuxedos and chefs' hats.

When Pierre and the Daumonts entered, the chefs
all rose to their feet in welcome and clapped.

"Monsieur Daumont," the president announced,
"it is an honor to have you and your party grace
our table at this auspicious occasion. Let the
banquet begin!"

A gong rang. Savory aromas floated through the air and Pierre's mouth began to water. He was seated at the head of the table, with Madame Daumont to the right of him and Monsieur Daumont at his left. The president of the chefs was at the other end. Henriette sat at a separate table with her piglets. Each chef had prepared his specialty. The dishes were charming to behold and most pleasing to smell.

"Ha! This looks good, wife," cried Monsieur Daumont. "Come, we must do it justice."

The menu consisted of truffle turnovers, truffles coddled in sweet cream, roast pheasant stuffed with truffles, truffle salad, and truffle pie, all washed down with champagne. Between each course the chefs refreshed their palates with lemon sherbet. It was a long time from the beginning of the feast until the end.

Throughout the meal, the chefs tasted, looked at each other, and complimented the dishes:

"A tasty mouthful," Monsieur Daumont remarked.

"Oh, dear sir, what a glorious crust," sighed Madame Daumont as she swallowed a delicious morsel of pie.

Pierre cleaned his plate. Ah, but life was good to him! He smiled over to his wife and blew her a kiss.

Four hours after they had sat down, the president stood up and began to speak:

"My fellow gastronomes, this is a night of triumph for the truffle, for Périgord, and for our guests of honor, the Daumonts and Master Pierre. For all Frenchmen know that the truffle is a treasure of the French kitchen, and many claim that France might fall without truffles."

"Hear! Hear!" shouted the chefs. The master chef held up his hand to silence them and went on:

"I would like to read the following proposal that I have drawn up for the president of the Republic:

"We, the Exclusive Circle of French Chefs, in the name of the French people, propose that November 1, the first day of the truffle season, be named Truffle Day, and that Pierre be the symbol of that day."

The hall shook with applause. Pierre felt dizzy from all the food and excitement. Monsieur Daumont and his wife, who were just simple folk from the provinces, were awed by the event.

"And now," the speaker continued, "we shall have a little concluding ceremony."

At this point, a waiter marched into the dining room bearing a silver tray covered with a white napkin. He carried the tray to the head of the table, where Pierre, pink of face, sat. At a nod from the president, another waiter whisked the napkin off the tray and underneath, in all its glory, lay a single huge truffle.

"Monsieur Daumont," continued the president, "do you think Pierre would do us the honor of consuming this pure truffle, the pride of Périgord, in our presence?"

Monsieur Daumont turned to Pierre.

"How about it, Pierre?" he asked.

Solemnly Pierre rose to his feet. Full though he was from the enormous dinner, he bowed low. Sniffing the truffle, he paused a moment, and then slowly, appreciatively, bit into it. He did not pounce on it like a greedy pig. That would have been an insult in such company. He kept nodding and smiling to show his approval. It was at its peak of flavor. When he was through, the dining room rang with cries of ''bravo,'' ''bravo.''

Suddenly a reporter appeared and snapped a picture of Pierre finishing the last bit of truffle, ears perked, tail curled with pleasure, and a chef's cap on his head. The piglets squealed with delight and scooted over to climb on his lap.

"May I propose a toast?" the president announced. He raised his glass of champagne. *"Vive la truffe pure,"* he cried.

All the chefs shouted: *"Vive la truffe pure,* long live the pure truffle. *Vive Pierre!"*